BULLYSAURUS

AND THE ALIEN

Damon Burnard

Hodder
Children's
Books

a division of Hodder Headline plc

This book is dedicated to all the kids,
parents and staff at PSED –
but especially the kids!

Copyright © 1999 Damon Burnard

First published in Great Britain in 1999 by
Hodder Children's Books

The right of Damon Burnad to be identified as the Author and
Illustrator of this Work has been asserted by him in accordance with
the Copyright, Designs and Patents Act 1988

10 9 8 7 6 5 4 3 2 1

A Catalogue record for this book is available from the British
Library.

ISBN 0340 74364 6

Printed and bound in Great Britain by
The Guernsey Press Co. Ltd., Guernsey, Channel Islands

Hodder Children's Books
A Division of Hodder Headline plc
338 Euston Road
London NW1 3BH

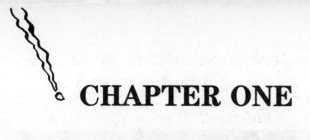

CHAPTER ONE

Suddenly . . .

CHAPTER TWO

Once opon a time, in a forest, on an island, in a swampy, steamy sea there lived a bunch of dinosaurs in happy harmony.

It was summer on the island. By day, it was too hot to do much but laze around, and at night it was too hot to sleep. Instead, the dinosaurs lay beneath the Hooter tree, listening to the chattering crickets, and counting the stars.

One night, Bullysaurus had got as far as eleven, when something caught his eye.

"Is it just me," he said, "or is that star moving?"

"Yes, it is!" Dolores cried, leaping to her feet.

Across the sky streaked a star. At first it was a distant speck, but it grew steadily bigger and brighter until it lit up the forest and threw shadows onto the ground.

"Oh my goodness!" gasped Dinah.

It's heading for our island!

Down sped the blazing star, closer and closer until . . . it crashed in the middle of the forest!

Dolores had an idea. "Hey!" she cried.

"Oh, I don't know," yawned Frank.

Tyrone and Terry agreed. But Bully, Dinah and Theo thought that an expedition into the forest was a fine idea.

"Great!" said Dolores.

CHAPTER THREE

The adventurers rose with the sun.
Dolores, Theo and Dinah gathered
together some provisions, while
Bully prepared some delicious
snacks to take on the journey.
When they were ready, the four
said goodbye to their friends, and
stepped bravely into the forest, to
begin their Great Expedition . . .

The further they walked into the forest, the deeper and darker it became. Their skin grew itchy and sticky, and bugs buzzed and crawled around them.

At last they came upon a little stream, and sat down for a rest.

"Phew!" sighed Dolores.

"Let's go home" moaned Theo.

"No way!" snapped Dinah.

On they went, further from the Hooter tree, with Dinah leading the way.

Suddenly she let out a shout.

"Hey! Come here! Quick!" she called.

Her friends hurried over. Before
them lay a clearing, covered in
peculiar shaped rocks and clouds of
steam. The air was filled with
bubbling and hissing sounds.

With Dolores in front and Theo grumbling at the rear, the dinosaurs tiptoed carefully past steaming springs and burping mud pools.

"Careful!" warned Dolores, guiding them around a great rock.

"I could have told you that, clever-clogs!" griped Theo, stopping to catch his breath. Suddenly he felt the ground around him tremble . . .

. . . and then . . .

Up he shot, high into the air, on
top of a great jet of water!

He'd stepped on a geyser, just as it had gushed!

Then, as quickly as it had started, the geyser stopped, and . . .

. . . down fell Theo, back to earth!

The others heard his shout and came rushing over.

"Oh, n – nothing" said Theo, who was feeling a little foolish. "Nothing at all."

"Well, thanks, but I can take care of myself" said Theo.

Soon the dinosaurs were back in the forest. It was growing late, and through the canopy of leaves they could see the moon rising. This time Bully took the lead, so he was the first to see it; something glowing and smouldering on the forest floor.

"What is it?" gasped Dolores.
"I – I don't know!" stuttered Bully.

CHAPTER FOUR

In front of them lay a mass of metal.

"What can it be?" whispered Dinah.

"Well", said Theo, importantly,

"It looks as if it's fallen from the sky!" said Dolores. "It must be what we saw last night!"

"Wow!" said Bully, reaching out to touch it.

Suddenly . . .

As if from nowhere, a flying
fruit smacked him in the face!

Bully turned and looked up into
a tree. And there he saw a most
incredible sight . . .

CHAPTER FIVE

Hopping angrily about on a branch was a strange creature. It had yellow skin, an oval face and two dangly things growing out of the top of its head.

"Leave my ship alone!" the creature yelled hurling down fruit.

GO AWAY!

"Hey, relax!" shouted Dinah.
"We're not going to hurt you . . . or
your thingummy!"

"You're sure?" said the creature.
"Yes!" insisted Dolores. "Honest!"

The creature wasn't certain . . .

. . . but he quickly changed his mind
when Bully opened his bundle and
laid out the delicious food he'd
prepared.

The creature crammed some
food into his mouth, spraying the
dinosaurs with crumbs.

"You're welcome!" smiled Dinah.

The dinosaurs watched and waited while the creature ate. When at last it had finished, it wiped its mouth and, in a quiet, shaky voice, began its story . . .

CHAPTER SIX

"My name is Zooble," it said,
pointing to the heap of metal . . .

Zooble told them how he'd been
caught in a shower of meteorites,
how his ship was struck, and
how he'd had to crash-land on the
dinosaurs' planet.

"Wow!" gasped Bully.

Suddenly Zooble looked embarrassed. "I can't quite remember," he said quietly. "I've been travelling so long, I've forgotten."

"So, where were you going, then?" asked Dinah.

Zooble blushed. "I – I don't really know!" he mumbled, "I've forgotten that, too!"

CHAPTER SEVEN

Zooble wandered over to the wrecked spacecraft and began pulling at some cables.

"That depends," he said impatiently.

"Then you are of no help at all!"
snapped Zooble. He turned his back
on the dinosaurs.

"Now listen!" replied Dinah, crossly.

Zooble stopped what he was doing. "Forgive me," he muttered. "I've been very rude. Now, if you'll excuse me . . ."

I've much work to do...

Well, OK... but we're here if you need us!

He thinks I'm stupid!

The dinosaurs left Zooble to himself, and lay down to rest in some long, cool grass. After a day of adventures they were tired. It wasn't long before they were all fast asleep . . .

CHAPTER EIGHT

A while later the dinosaurs woke to the sound of Zooble bolting, and fusing, and soldering and riveting.

"Can't sleep," muttered Zooble.

While Zooble worked, the dinosaurs decided to explore the forest. Even though they had found what they were looking for they didn't want to return home just yet.

And anyway, they wanted to see what would happen with Zooble . . .

The days passed. When he wasn't working on the ship, Zooble was drawing complicated diagrams filled with complicated sums.

Theo pretended to understand.

"Oh, of course!" blushed Theo, walking away.

Whenever the evening came around, Bully lit a fire and barbecued all the delicacies he'd found during the day.

At first the dinosaurs had to
persuade Zooble to join them,
but it wasn't long before he
was sitting with them around
the fire, listening to their jokes
and stories. And then he told
them of his travels; tales of
giant space serpents, three-
headed beasts, and the Planet
of Singing Magicians.

The dinosaurs gaped in wonder.

CHAPTER NINE

One evening, Zooble made an announcement.

"After much toil, I have rebuilt my ship," he said.

The dinosaurs tried hard to sound glad and happy for Zooble . . .

The truth was, they were sad to see him go.

The next morning, Zooble jumped into his spacecraft. "Farewell!" he said with a bow.

He pressed a button and pulled a lever. Flames spat, and the engine spluttered.

So much smoke billowed and belched about, that the dinosaurs couldn't see past their noses.

BANG! **SCREECH!** _fizz!_

Something screeched, and fizzed and loudly banged. And then there was silence.

"He may have been rude and grumpy," said Dolores,

But I'll miss Zooble just the same!

Splutter!

Cough!

"So what you need," said Dolores, "is a kind of push?"

"A push?" scoffed Theo.

But Zooble agreed with Dolores. "Exactly right!" he said.

Straight away, they got down to the very important business of Zooble's jump-start . . .

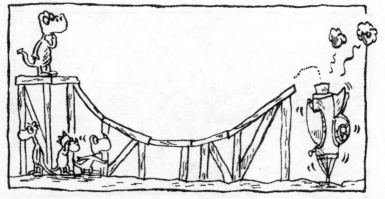

However hard they tried, nothing seemed to work.

They had run out of ideas and were losing hope, when Theo – who'd been very quiet – cleared his throat

Ahem!

"I've got an idea!" he said, shyly.

But it's probably stupid and not clever at all — just like me!

"Nonsense, Theo!" said Dinah.

Tell us, please!

What is it, Theo?

Theo thought for a moment.
"I'm not sure I can tell you," he said.

But maybe I could show you, instead?

CHAPTER ELEVEN

Theo led the dinosaurs through
the forest. At last they came to a
clearing, filled with steam, and lava,
and bubbling mud pools.

"This way!" said Theo, leading them over to a hole in the ground.

Having no ideas left of their own, the dinosaurs and Zooble pushed and heaved until the ship was in the hole, its nose pointing to the sky.

"And what do we do now?"
asked Zooble, impatiently.

"Er . . . we wait!" said Theo.

And so they waited . . .

. . . and waited.

They were about to give up, when
suddenly the ground began to tremble
and shake.

And then . . .

Up gushed a great tower of water,
shooting Zooble's ship into the sky!

Zooble tugged at the controls . . .

. . . and his engines roared to life!

Zooble turned somersaults in the air and swooped over the dinosaurs' heads.

"It worked!" he cried. "Thank you!"

"You're welcome!" yelled Theo, swelling with pride.

"We'll miss you!" cried Dolores over the roar of the engines.

Zooble waved and then up he flew, like a flaming arrow, until all that was left was a wisp of smoke, drifting in the blue summer sky.

CHAPTER TWELVE

The dinosaurs decided that tonight
would be their last in the forest,
before returning home to the Hooter
tree.

For the first time in a long while,
it felt cold after the sun went down.
Gloomily they sat around the
campfire, each thinking about Zooble
and how much they'd miss him.

To take his mind off such sad thoughts, Bullysaurus began to count the stars. He'd got as far as twelve, when something caught his eye.

"Hey! Look!" he gasped.

"He's right!" cried Dinah.

As the star fell closer it grew bigger and brighter, until at last the dinosaurs could see that it wasn't a star at all.

Suddenly, Theo jumped into the air.

HE'S BACK!

Down swooped the spaceship,
and out leapt Zooble!

He rushed over to the dinosaurs,
hugging each one in turn.

"I was a thousand light-years
away when I remembered what I
was looking for!" he sobbed joyfully.

"And what was that?" asked Dinah.

"Home!" cried Zooble, throwing his arms open wide.

CHAPTER THIRTEEN

After a night of joyous celebration, the dinosaurs and Zooble made their way back to the Hooter tree.

Frank, Terry and Tyrone were surprised to see a small, yellow-faced stranger walking with their friends.

Warmly, they shook his hand.
"He's very clever you know!"
added Theo quietly.

When Zoary heard that he
grinned and shook his head.

"I'm clever enough to have learned that we're all clever," he laughed,

And so ended the dinosaurs' Great Expedition. They left to find a fallen star and found a friend, instead . . .

If you're ever fortunate enough to
visit Yellowstone Park in the USA,
you'll find a geyser. Nowadays
it's called Old Faithful, but it's the
same one that Theo found, all those
years ago. So think of him, if you
remember, and of Zooble, too, for
if it wasn't for that geyser he might
never have left. And if Zooble had
never left, he'd never have found
his way home . . .